INVINCIBLES
The HAMSTER RESCUE

The INVINCIBLES

Caryl Hart
Sarah Warburton

nosy
crow

The Invincibles' World!
Big
Nell's house
stores
CINEMA
Shops
BIG CITY
Bus Station
flats

For Diddy Marvin, wherever you may be.
Thanks x
C. H.

For Blazer, the King of hamsters.
S. W.

First published in the UK in 2016 by Nosy Crow Ltd
The Crow's Nest, 10a Lant Street
London, SE1 1QR, UK

Nosy Crow and associated logos are trademarks and/or registered
trademarks of Nosy Crow Ltd

1 3 5 7 9 10 8 6 4 2

A CIP catalogue record for this book will be available from the British Library.

Printed in Spain

Papers used by Nosy Crow are made from wood grown in
sustainable forests.

ISBN: 978 0 85763 792 5

www.nosycrow.com

The HAMSTER RESCUE

You'd never think that a hamster could save
you from anything. But I'm telling you, our
school hamster, Hamish, saved me from the
Worst Mistake of my Life. He actually did!
It all started with – well – you'll see.

Chapter One
I Live in a House

The first thing you need to know about me is my name. It's Nell. Nell Henry. I'm not sure whether to tell you my full name, because I don't know you very well yet, and you might tell someone like Lucy Perkins. That would be a total disaster, if you ask me. She'd probably parade round the playground with her stupid friends chanting it over and over and laughing. Why do people *do* that? It's not as if I've ever done anything to her.

Anyway. I'm Nell and, like most people, I live in a house with my family. We're not poor. Or rich. We're just normal.

My dad goes to work and my mum supposedly works at home. She says she's Building Up A Business making old-fashioned party stuff, but she seems to spend more time untangling the baby from strings of bunting than she does working.

Once she lost the baby completely. Turns out she'd taped it into a cardboard box with someone's order by mistake. Imagine if she'd actually posted it!

Chapter Two
Bunting's for Girls

So the other day me and Freddie Spoon were in the den in Mrs Next Door's garden, and Freddie Spoon was acting really weird. Freddie Spoon has been my best friend ever since that day at nursery school when I accidentally spilled tadpoles all over the carpet. I'd been trying to help a poorly

one, but when I'd put the net in,
loads of others had jumped in
with him. Because I was only little,
I thought it would be a good idea
to tip them out on the carpet to sort
them out! It was Freddie Spoon that
saved them all – and me!

After we'd got them all back
into the tank, Freddie Spoon
pretended to the teacher that
the wet patch on the carpet
was because he'd had a "little
accident"! Instead of telling
me off, the teacher took
Freddie Spoon to the
lost-property box to find
some dry pants and shorts,
and gave us both a chocolate
drop for being brave. After
that we just sort of became
friends.

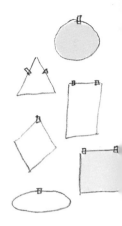

Normally me and Freddie Spoon can't stop talking, but that day in Mrs Next Door's garden he was all sort of quiet and shy. He kept digging at the ground with a piece of stick and not looking at me.

So I got the chalk out from our Tin of Useful Things and started rewriting our sign. It says:

the
Invincibles
Keep Out

The Invincibles. That's us. Me and Freddie Spoon. If you're invincible it means that you can't be hurt or killed or anything. Even if you're in a fire, you can just walk out of the flames and not be even a tiny bit burned. I told Freddie Spoon that I was going to draw flames on our sign but he didn't even look up. He just poke-poke-poked at the mud with his piece of stick and scowled.

I was about to ask him what was wrong when he said, "You know it's my birthday on Friday? Well, my mum says Dad might be coming back so I'm going to have a party. She says I can invite some friends, so you can come if you want."

I stared at him. In all the years and years I've known him, Freddie Spoon has never EVER had a birthday party. I don't know why, really; probably because he has lots of brothers and sisters and can't fit anyone else into his house.

I was going to say yes, but Freddie Spoon kept gabbling on. "You don't have to come if you don't want to 'cos it'll be a bit of a squash and we'll probably only have shop cake and packet ham sandwiches and stuff, but. . ."

I squatted down and punched him on the arm. I said, "Of course I'll come, you big wally! I bet Mum's got some cool birthday bunting you can have."

Freddie Spoon said, "You've got to be kidding! Bunting's for girls." But he was grinning from ear to ear.

Chapter Three
All About Dads

We spent the rest of the afternoon fixing
the roof of our den. After a while Mrs Next
Door came out in her wheelchair and gave
us some chocolate biscuits and juice.

I said, "So what do you want for your
birthday? It's only a few days away."

Freddie Spoon said, "I'd love a new
bike 'cos mine's much too small, but Mum
says she's not sure because she's had to
buy shoes for Maisy and Daisy now that
they're walking." Maisy and Daisy are
Freddie Spoon's twin sisters.

I said that didn't sound fair. Freddie
Spoon said he wasn't that bothered but I
could tell he was putting on a brave face,
so to change the subject I said, "I bet
you're looking forward to seeing your dad
though."

Freddie Spoon beamed. "He's been away six whole months this time." He sounded proud. Freddie Spoon's dad works on an oil rig in the middle of the sea. He goes under the water in a diving suit and fixes things with a special underwater tool kit.

SPECIAL UNDERWATER TOOL KIT

I said, "I wish *I* had your dad. *My* dad just sits in an office all day drawing pipes and staircases. He's so boring."

Freddie Spoon said, "I'll swap you. You can have a dad who's away all the time, and I'll have a dad who tells jokes at teatime and takes me swimming at the weekends." I said I'd think about it. But I wasn't so sure I wanted to swap any more.

I said, "Do you think he misses you?"

Freddie Spoon pulled a lump of moss off a tree and threw it over the fence into the woods. He said, "I dunno." Then he said, "S'pose so. Yeah." He stood there like he was thinking about something, then he ripped off another lump of moss and threw it at me. We spent the rest of the afternoon chucking moss and sticks over the fence and at each other.

Chapter Four

Big Brothers are a Pain

Have you got a big brother? Mine's called Lucas. He's the most irritating thing in the whole universe. He thinks he's cool because he's got long floppy hair and wears too-big trousers that keep falling down so you can

see his pants. I think
he's stupid because he spends
hours in the bathroom squeezing his
spots and spraying himself with Pit Stop
deodorant because he thinks it will make
girls like him.

Normally on a Saturday night, me and my dad and my granny make popcorn and watch *X-Factor* on TV. My granny lives in the flat at the bottom of our house, but she comes to visit us all the time so she's not lonely. I've never met my grandad. Granny says he's off climbing a volcano in Indonesia. He must be a slow walker because it's taken him over nine years so far.

Anyway, we were just settling down with our popcorn when the sound of the TV was totally drowned out by this terrible wailing upstairs. I jumped so much my popcorn exploded all over the living-room carpet. My granny leapt up shouting, "Call the police! Somebody is strangling a cat!"

But my dad just sat there laughing. "That's not a cat, Margaret," he said. "That's your grandson."

"Well, what does he think he's doing?" said my granny. "Is he in pain?"

I grabbed a couple of cushions and clamped them over my ears. "He soon will be if he doesn't stop that terrible racket," I grumbled.

My dad laughed. "I think that noise is what he and his friends call singing," he said. "They're practising for their first concert next week."

A concert? So my big brother Lucas and his nerdy friends are going to stand up in front of actual people, wailing like crazed lunatics while strumming and blowing instruments they don't even know the names of? They'd better not make *me* go and watch!

But my granny was beaming. "Ooh, how lovely," she said. "My Bertie and I had some fun times when we were on tour, I can tell you!" Her eyes went all starry and watery. "He played guitar and I was the drummer. Oh yes, those were the days!"

I stared at my granny. "You were a *drummer* in a *band?*" I gasped. "I didn't know they even had music in those days!"

"Oh yes!" my granny smiled. "Music was everything in the sixties, you know. Oh, the things I could tell you…" I wanted to hear more but my dad coughed and said in a very loud voice, "Perhaps Lucas and his friends should go on *X-Factor?*"

"Good idea," I said. "Then we could turn them off."

The next morning I said, "So where's your Big Concert, superstar? Sunny View Home for the Elderly? Nowheres-ville Village Hall?" Lucas shovelled cornflakes into his mouth and buried his head in his *Skull Man* comic.

"It's not a concert, stupid. It's a *gig*. And for your information," he snapped, "we're playing at a very exclusive venue AND we're getting PAID!"

I was so surprised, my half-chewed breakfast erupted out of my mouth and splattered across the table. "You're saying someone's going to actually PAY you to deafen every living person within three miles?"

Lucas smirked meanly. "Yep. And I'm going to spend all the money on sweets and I'm not going to give you ANY." Then he got up from the table and huffed off.

See? I told you big brothers are a pain.

Chapter Five
I Am Chosen

When I got to school on Monday, most of the other kids were clustered together at the back of the class. Miss Sweetly wasn't there yet so I sat in my place and ate my sandwiches. Freddie Spoon came in with Hamish and plonked his cage on Miss Sweetly's desk. Me and Freddie Spoon are going to be Extreme Wildlife Experts when we grow up – like that man on the telly who picks up scorpions and poisonous spiders and things. We know that looking after the school hamster isn't quite as exciting, but it's something that we do at weekends. You know, to get in practice.

Suddenly, Cally Thompson started squealing with delight and waving a piece of paper in the air. Other children peeled away from the huddle, smiling broadly, and there in the middle was Lucy Perkins. She was handing out birthday invitations.

A few kids still hovered nervously, hoping they were good enough to be honoured with a golden ticket to the Party of the Year. I got my reading book out and pretended not to care whether I was invited or not. But secretly I was hoping and hoping that one of those sparkly pink envelopes had my name on it. The room hummed with excitement as the Chosen Ones discussed what they were going to wear and what presents they were going to buy the Birthday Girl. I took a deep breath and tried not to imagine what I would be missing.

And then the impossible happened. It actually did! Lucy Perkins came right up to me and shoved an envelope between my nose and my book!

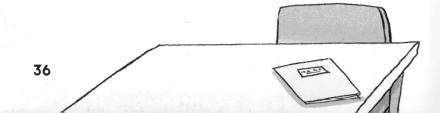

Dear Nell

Please come to my Birthday Party on Friday 16th, 4pm – 6pm.

Pony Rides
Nail Painting and Makeovers by Luscious

Lucky Dip
Pass the Parcel
Prizes
Birthday tea

PLUS: special appearance by local band
The Zombies

RSVP: Sandra Perkins, The Manor, 12
Fitzherbert Avenue.

I couldn't believe it! Lucy Perkins had invited me to her party.

ME!

I thought she hated me, but I must have been wrong all this time. Then suddenly my bubble of happiness popped. What was I going to buy her? It would have to be something really special, some earrings perhaps, or … or … oh, crikey! What *do* you buy someone like Lucy Perkins? She'd probably expect a gold bracelet or a DVD box set or something.

I turned to Freddie Spoon. "I'll never save up enough money by Friday!" Freddie Spoon was about to say something when Miss Sweetly came in.

"Settle down, children," she said. "Let's take the register." And that was that.

Chapter Six
The True Value of a Gift

When I got home Mum was decorating the
Baby with chocolate icing and sprinkles.
She wasn't doing it on purpose, obviously,
but decorating cakes is always a challenge
when you have a baby helping out.

I flopped miserably into a chair, grabbed the icing bowl and dipped my finger into it.

Mum smiled at me. "Hey, grumpy chops, what's up?" I licked my finger, reached into my bag and showed her the invitation. Mum looked confused. "But that's lovely," she said. "And the Perkinses are such a ... err ... such a ... *popular* family.

Lots of people seem to like them. In fact, Mrs Perkins has asked me to make Lucy's birthday cake. She even offered to pay me, but I said I wouldn't hear of it!"

I said, "But what am I going to buy her? Lucy Perkins is not the sort of person who's going to be happy with a stationery set or some hair bobbles!"

Mum said, "The true value of a gift is not about how much it costs, love. It's about how much thought you put into choosing it."

I said, "You try telling that to Lucy Perkins."

But Mum just smiled. "Why don't you make her some biscuits and decorate them? You're so good at that sort of thing."

And I thought that was not such a bad idea.

Chapter Seven
The Worst Person in the Whole Wide World

I didn't see much of Freddie Spoon for the rest of the week, but I didn't really mind because I was so busy looking up recipes for the perfect icing and planning cool designs to put on my biscuits. Lucas spent the week locked in his bedroom with his friends, practising for his Big Gig.

I baked the biscuits on Wednesday. The third batch came out pretty well, with only a few burned bits at the edges. Mum said it's best to let them cool overnight, so I had to wait till after school on Thursday to get on with the decorating.

As I was walking
home I spotted
Freddie Spoon
whizzing along on his
brother's bike. It was so big
that he had to stand on the pedals.
Even so, he streaked past me at about
a hundred miles an hour.

"Hey, Freddie Spoon!" I called. "Wait!"

Freddie Spoon stopped, turned and
cycled slowly back towards me.

I said, "Do you want to come to mine?
I'm decorating biscuits for Lucy's party.
You can help if you want." But Freddie
Spoon just shrugged.

So I said, "Cheer up, misery-guts! Your
dad'll be home tomorrow and then it's
your … your…" Freddie Spoon looked
at me and suddenly I felt like the worst
person in the whole wide world.

"OH, FREDDIE SPOON!" My face felt hot and my hands went all sweaty. "Oh, Freddie Spoon," I said. "I am SO sorry!"

Freddie Spoon's dad was going to come home the next day because the next day was going to be Freddie Spoon's FIRST and ONLY EVER birthday party. The party I said I'd go to. The party I *want* to go to. But now I've gone and told Lucy Perkins that I'll go to *her* party too! And I've made her a present and everything!

"I can't believe I've done such a stupid thing!"

But Freddie Spoon said, "It doesn't bother me *whose* party you go to." He started fiddling with the front light on his brother's bike, muttering under his breath, "Stupid battery must've gone…"

"But, Freddie," I said. "I want to come to yours!"

Freddie stopped fiddling with the light and glared at me. "Well, my dad's not even coming now. He's got some emergency on the rigs, so I'm not even going to bother." He said parties were for babies anyway. He said I might as well go to Lucy's because I'd only be bored at his house. Then he pushed on the pedals and cycled away.

I called after him, "Are you sure you don't mind?" But he didn't answer. "Oh well," I shrugged. "I guess it's for the best."

Chapter Eight
Wayne's Drains

I thought I was in trouble when I saw the Wayne's Drains van parked outside my house on Friday after school. Surely I hadn't blocked the toilet again!

I still can't believe Mum and Dad blamed me for the last time it happened. I reckon it was their fault for getting me to clear up the supper things in the first place. How could

I have known that leftover fish and chips aren't actually flushable?

It was my turn to have Hamish for the weekend, so I put his cage down on the pavement and tried to think. He came out of his little plastic house and started running around his wheel without a care in the world. Sometimes I wish I was a hamster.

I was trying to decide whether to go inside, or make a run for it, when Lucas came staggering out of the front door carrying a large black box thing that looked a bit like a television with no screen. He dumped it on the pavement next to the van then hurried back into the house. The next minute his two weird friends came out with bundles of wires and gizmos and a beaten-up old keyboard that I've never seen before.

Then a thin, beardy-looking man – Wayne, I guess – helped load everything into the van. My big brother Lucas and his friends climbed in too. For a second I thought they might be being kidnapped, but when Mum and the Baby came out to wave, I realised with a sigh that they were probably just off to the Big Gig.

Did you know that lots of people spend literally *hours* getting ready to go out to parties and things? I don't know *what* they do, because it only ever takes me five minutes, tops.

Hamish was climbing up the bars of his cage, so I took him out for a cuddle. He sat on his haunches  and licked his paws. Then he reached up behind his head and swooshed his paws over his ears towards his nose. That's how hamsters have a wash! I said, "There's no point YOU getting all jazzed up, Hamish. You're not coming to the party!" Hamish stopped washing and looked at me longingly with his shiny black eyes. I stroked his silky nose, feeling like a meanie. "Well, I suppose I *could* take you…" I said doubtfully. "But you'll have to promise to stay in my pocket and not get lost." Hamish said he would definitely stay in my pocket. So that was settled.

I did a twirl for Mum, and she said I looked super-jazzy. Then I played peepo with the Baby until it was time to go.

Chapter Nine
The Party of the Year

As Mum's car crunched up the gravel drive,
I gazed out of the window. There was a
sort of miniature circus tent in the garden
with two little ponies tied up outside. Their
manes and tails were plaited with ribbons
and a lady was busy brushing their soft,

shiny coats. Another lady was setting up a face-painting area, and a third was filling a table with hundreds of bottles of nail varnish and glitter glue and make-up. Now, I'm not really a *girly* girl, but I couldn't help feeling excited at the thought of getting all glammed up and riding a real pony.

But the minute we walked into Lucy Perkins's house I knew I'd made my First Big Mistake. I stood gawping on the doorstep but Mum was right behind me carrying the cake, so I didn't have much choice but to go inside. Mum squeezed past me and took the cake into the kitchen.

I stepped on to the cream carpet, feeling suddenly shy and very small.

You see, all the other girls were skipping around in sparkly skirts and crop tops and clip-cloppy shoes. They all looked so grown up and flouncy and pretty. I stared down at my leopard-print leggings and new purple trainers and felt a bit queasy. Lucy Perkins tottered over, her arm linked through Cally Thompson's in what looked like a wobbly sort of three-legged race.

"What's *she* doing here?" Cally Thompson said in a loud voice.

Lucy Perkins looked me up and down and wrinkled her nose. "My mother *made* me invite her. She said it would be rude not to, since her mum was making my cake. I wanted a butterfly one from Harrington's but my mum says shop cakes are common. I'm not touching anything that's come out of *her* house. It's probably got *things* crawling in it." Then to me she said, "I told my mum you wouldn't want to come because you don't have any nice clothes. But she said you could probably find something half decent in the charity shop."

Cally Thompson said, "Guess they didn't have anything in your size." Then she and Lucy Perkins collapsed in a pile of giggles.

I was going to say that charity shops are great because you can get really nice things for not much money and help other people at the same time. And it's recycling. But Lucy Perkins didn't give me a chance to speak. She said, "My mum said I have to be nice to you because you don't have any friends, apart from that awful Freddie Fork or whatever his name is."

My tummy went all stirry then, and my cheeks began to burn. I said, "His name's Freddie *Spoon*," but that just made them laugh even more.

Then they started making kissing noises and pretending to faint. "Ooh! Watch out, everyone! Smelly Nelly's in Luuurve!"

I wanted to thump her then, but Mum and Mrs Perkins came back out of the kitchen, so I couldn't. Mrs Perkins pretend-kissed my mum saying, "Mwa! Mwa!" in a really loud and show-offy way.

Mum nudged me with her elbow and said, "Have fun." And then she left.

Mrs Perkins looked down at me with a sort of tiny frown. Then she did a really fake smile and said, "Oh, Antonnnnella! How laaarvely to see you. SO glad you could come and what un*uuus*ual leggings."

O.M.G!

As if things weren't bad enough already. Why did she have to go and call me Antonella in front of everyone?!

65

Mrs Perkins gestured towards the parcel I was still holding. "What do you say, Lucy daaarling?"

Lucy snatched the parcel, saying, "Thank you, Antonnnnella!" in a voice like her mother's.

She ripped off the paper and opened the tin inside. The look on her face told me that I'd just made my Second Big Mistake.

"They're biscuits," I stuttered stupidly. "I – I made them."

Lucy Perkins pulled a face, as if she'd just opened a tin of decorated doggy-do. "Well, I'm sure *someone* will eat them." She thrust the tin back at me, then she and Cally Thompson linked arms again and tottered off giggling and chanting, "Nell and Freddie, sitting in a tree, k.i.s.s.i.n.g!"

That's IT! I thought. *I'm going home!* I yanked open the front door, and marched into the garden. But the car wasn't there. Mum had gone.

Chapter Ten
Stampede!

The Perkinses' huge living room was filled with clusters of girls, all giggling and chattering with excitement. At one end was a long table piled with fancy-looking presents. I hid my embarrassing biscuit tin right at the back, then lifted Hamish gently out of my pocket and let him walk over my hands. I kept swapping my hands over so that he kept on walking and walking like he was on a conveyor belt. Hamish thought he was going on a fantastic adventure. He didn't know he wasn't really going anywhere!

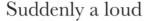

Suddenly a loud

KERAANNGGG!

blasted from another room. It made me
jump! Hamish fell off my hands and landed
on the carpet. I bet you think hamsters are
slow runners because their legs are so short.
But I'm telling you, that hamster could
shift!

I dropped to the floor, ready to scuttle
after him, but was overtaken by a sparkling
stampede of over-excited nine-year-olds
rushing past me towards the play room.
If it wasn't for my quick thinking and
expert knowledge of enemy-
evasion techniques, I'd
have been crushed to
death for sure.

"The Zombies are here!"

"Save a place for me at the front!"

"This is so cool!"

"Ladies and ... err ... ladies," boomed a voice. "We are The Zombies. Welcome to our first ever live—"

WHHHHEEEEEEPPPP! A loud screech from the speakers drowned out the next few words. Even so, something about that voice sounded familiar.

I crawled around the empty living room, searching frantically for Hamish, hoping against hope that he had survived the stampede. But Hamish was nowhere to be seen.

Chapter Eleven

Zombie Attack
– and a "Rat"

KERANNGG! The band launched into their first song. It was ear-crackingly loud and sounded like a deranged elephant being attacked by a herd of braying donkeys.

It. Was.

AWFUL!

But that didn't stop Lucy Perkins and her friends from screaming their heads off in a frenzy. Suddenly the crowd surged forwards

and the lead singer was knocked right off
his feet! Immediately he was buried in a
frantic knot of over-keen schoolgirls. After
a terrifying struggle, Cally Thompson
emerged from the bundle waving his jacket
in the air, a triumphant grin on her face.
And then the room was filled with an ear-
splitting scream.

Everyone froze. Lucy Perkins stood in the middle of the room, her hair all mussed up from scrambling through the crowds, one of her sparkly heels missing. She was as white as a sheet, her eyes were all goggly and from her mouth came a scream even more piercing than the feedback from the microphones.

"A rat!" she screamed.
"There's a

RAT

in my house!" She raised
a trembling arm and
pointed towards a
posh sofa thing.

The room erupted into even more chaos than before. It was actually quite funny, in a scary sort of way. Girls jumped up on the chairs and tables, or ran around the room screeching as if the place was about to be buried in molten lava and ash like what happened when that volcano erupted in Pompeii!

The band members took their chance to escape, grabbing their battered instruments and dodging out of the room.

"Run for it!" shouted one.

"Every man for himself!" shouted another.

I dived underneath the sofa thing, scooped Hamish up and placed him safely back in my pocket. But as I was backing out, someone grabbed my ankle. "Get off me!" I growled, kicking hard. "I've got a RAT and I'm not afraid to use it!"

"Owwww!" yelped the person. "Hey! Nell! It's me!"

"Me who?"

"*Me* me! Get me out of here!"

"Lucas?" I was so astonished, I clutched at his arms, gawping. "But you're at… Why are you…" And then it dawned on me. "The Zombies is *your* band?" I gasped. "And this – *this* is your Big Gig?!"

Lucas looked at me pleadingly. "Please, Nell. Just get me out of here! They're going to eat me alive!"

Chapter Twelve

Escape With Cake

Suddenly I knew exactly what to do. I grabbed my tin of biscuits and the party bag with my name on it and dragged Lucas towards the kitchen. "Get the cake!" I yelled.

Lucas gawped at the array of fancy pastries, cakes and sweets on the table, unsure what to do. "Come on," I hissed. "Mum spent ages making it and I'm not going to let it get wasted on that stuck-up, spangle-headed snake. She'll never even notice it's gone." Lucas grabbed the towering creation and we tore out of the front door and down the drive.

"Wait for us!" Lucas and I stopped in our tracks. At the end of the drive was a quivering, talking bush!

"Yikes!" I cried. "A talking bush!" But of course it wasn't. It was Lucas's nerdy friends. They scrambled out of the bush and clung to Lucas.

"Follow Nell," said Lucas. Then we all legged it.

But we didn't run home. Oh no. I had a much better plan.

"Where are we going?" gasped Lucas, struggling under the weight of the tottering cake.

"Yeah," puffed his nerdy friends. "Where ARE we going?"

"Somewhere we should have gone in the first place," I grinned. "Come on."

Chapter Thirteen
The Best Birthday

It was Freddie Spoon's mum who opened the door. She had the twins, Maisy and Daisy, balanced on her hips.

"Mell!" cried Maisy. Or Daisy, I'm not sure which.

"Goodness me!" smiled Mrs Spoon. "Just look at the size of that cake! I thought you were at a party this evening."

My face went all hot and I looked at the floor. "We were," I said. "But, well, it didn't really... Maybe we could...?"

Mrs Spoon opened the door wide. "Come in, lassie," she said. "And bring your friends, though how you're all going to fit in is anybody's guess."

Freddie Spoon and his big brothers were crammed around the table, eating beans on toast.

"Give us a hand, will you?" said Lucas from behind the cake. Freddie's biggest brother, Jimmy, took the cake, while his second brother Timmy made a space. "A *rainbow* cake," he grinned. "Very nice!"

I shuffled up to Freddie Spoon but I couldn't look at him. Instead I got Hamish out of my pocket and fed him a bit of biscuit. He stuffed it into his cheek and sniffed around for more. Freddie Spoon gave him a bit of breadstick, and Hamish stuffed that in as well. He DID look funny!

"Lucy Perkins's party not quite up to scratch then?" said Freddie Spoon.

"Not even close," I said.

Then Freddie Spoon punched me on the arm. "What do you say then?"

"Sorry about your party."

"No, you idiot," said Freddie Spoon. "Say Happy Birthday!"

I looked up then, straight into my best friend's sparkly eyes and wondered how I could have been so stupid. No amount of pony rides or makeovers or lucky dips or party bags could ever replace an afternoon with Freddie Spoon and his mad family. "Happy birthday, Freddie Spoon!" I grinned.

Then me and Lucas and his nerdy friends told Mrs Spoon and Jimmy and Timmy and Freddie and his other brother Eddie all about Lucy Perkins and her terrible party. After we'd polished off our beans on toast, I handed round my biscuits. "Lucy Perkins doesn't eat biscuits," I said.

"More fool her," laughed Mrs Spoon.

"More, more!" squeaked Maisy and Daisy.

After tea, when we were stuffed to the brim, I helped Eddie clear up the dishes, while Maisy and Daisy showed off their new walking skills. Then we flopped on to the sofa and let Hamish run across our laps.

Suddenly the front door flew open and in walked a burly man, covered from head to foot in tattoos. "Freddie!" boomed the man.

Freddie Spoon jumped up and threw himself into the man's huge arms. "Dad!"

Mr Spoon lifted Freddie up and whirled him around. "Happy birthday, son!"

"I thought you weren't coming!" gasped Freddie Spoon. "Mum said they needed you on the oil rig."

Mr Spoon ruffled Freddie's hair and set him down. "They did," he smiled. "But I had something much more important to do." He nodded towards something in the front yard.

"A bike?!" gasped Freddie. "But I thought—"

Mr Spoon grinned. "The lads helped me fix it up for you. What do you think?"

"I think it's AWESOME!" said Freddie Spoon.

Chapter Fourteen
And the Band Played

Freddie's dad had a great big cup of tea and a great big slice of Mum's cake. Then he disappeared upstairs and came back down with a tiny little pink guitar.

"Come on then, boys," he boomed. "Let's have a knees-up!" He started strumming the little pink guitar and singing in a deep, mellow voice:

"They say it's your birthday, well, whadda you know…

"Come on, boys, join in! It's D-A-G. . ."

Lucas and the rest of the Zombies picked up their instruments and slowly started to strum the chords. Freddie's dad started the song again.

"They say it's your birthday, well,
whadda you know?
A birthday is there to mark
how you grow!
So raise up your voices and
pick up your feet
And dance with me to the birthday beat!
The birthday beat! The birthday beat!
Yeah Yeah Yeah!
The birthday BEAT!"

As the Zombies got the hang of it, the song got louder and louder and faster and faster. The brothers jumped up and started doing this crazy dancing and it was so funny that me and Freddie Spoon joined in. Soon we were all singing and dancing and stamping our feet and having a grand old time.

Freddie looked at me with his sparkly eyes and grinned. "This is the best birthday ever!" he said.

I kissed Hamish on his little pink nose and smiled back at Freddie Spoon. "Yes," I said. "It most certainly is!"

the End